MYSTERY SHORT STORY COLLECTION VOLUME 2

CONNOR WHITELEY

No part of this book may be reproduced in any form or by any electronic or mechanical means. Including information storage, and retrieval systems, without written permission from the author except for the use of brief quotations in a book review.

This book is NOT legal, professional, medical, financial or any type of official advice.

Any questions about the book, rights licensing, or to contact the author, please email connorwhiteley@connorwhiteley.net

Copyright © 2022 CONNOR WHITELEY

All rights reserved.

DEDICATION
Thank you to all my readers without you I couldn't do what I love.

AUTHOR OF BETTIE ENGLISH PRIVATE EYE SERIES

CONNOR WHITELEY

COOKIE THIEF

A JANE SMITH AMATEUR SLEUTH MYSTERY SHORT STORY

COOKIE THIEF

If there was one thing Jane Smith loved about the springtime, it was the Cookie Festival in her little village in the south of England. It was utterly amazing how the entire village smelt of the most amazing cookies in the entire country, Jane loved the massive hints of peanut, chocolate and even brandy in the air.

The entire village was a wonderful symphony of the senses, and Jane just loved it.

As she stood on the wonderful warm stone floor of her little kitchen, she whipped up her batter in her favourite cream bowl. Even the mixing up of the ingredients was enough to get Jane excited about the festival, even now she could hear all the kids running up and down the hills, houses and roads to see if any windows were open for their little hands to steal any cookies.

That was probably the one thing Jane's mother had forced into her, Jane was never ever allowed to put her cookies by the window to cool, otherwise little thieving hands would make them disappear.

In reality Jane loved the children in the village too much not to give them something, so as soon as a batch of cookies went wrong Jane put them on her large wooden window seal for the children to grab.

As she continued to whip up her cookie batter, Jane couldn't help but smile at all the fun memories of stealing cookies herself as a child. It was a strange tradition and game she would play with her friends, she thankfully always got more cookies than her friends to their annoyance, and her joy!

The most amazing wave of peanut butter cookies washed over Jane from the window making her taste the sweet sugar, creamy peanut butter and rich soft texture on her tongue.

Jane might not have known who they were coming from but she really wanted to find out. It was probably her next door neighbour Julie, she and Jane's mother would talk for hours about the perfect cookie, and Jane loved listening to the conversations.

Today Jane had to do her mother proud and win the contest for the Village's best cookies, and she really, really wanted that apron.

Jane's kids, Toby and Ross, might have said wanting an apron was such an old person's thing but Jane didn't care, she had to have that wonderful red, blue and golden apron. It would make her mother proud and Jane would be the talk of the village at last!

Jane picked up a cold box of chocolate chips and poured them generously into the batter and gave them a final mix.

"You in there Jane?" an elderly frail woman said from the window.

Jane gave her batter a final stir and went over to the window where a little old lady (and Jane's best friend) was leaning against as she caught her breath.

"You okay Marg?" Jane asked.

Jane's eyes narrowed on her best friend who wore her normal dull gardening clothes, fake pearl necklace and oversized pink hat.

"Yea pet just walked up the hill," Marg said looking around. "Are you alone?"

Jane smiled. It was a bit weird that Marg would even ask such a thing, she knew Toby and Ross were far away living with their wives and families and weren't coming to visit, Mr Smith was dead three years now, and she was baking which she always did alone.

"Sure. Walk round the front and come in for some cookies," Jane said.

Marg's eyes widened. "No. No. No, pet. I can't that's the problem,"

Jane leant closer to the window.

"Pet, the apron's gone!" Marg said.

Jane's mouth just dropped. How could the apron just be gone? She wanted to win that more than anything else in the world, the apron couldn't be gone.

"Someone stole it?" Jane said randomly.

Marg nodded. "Yea Pet. It's gone. You have to

help me find it,"

Then Jane remembered Marg was Head Judge this year for the festival, so everything about the contest was on her (rather ancient) head. A tiny part of Jane wondered whether Marg had simply misplaced it, it hadn't even been a week since she last had to go and help Marg find her glasses.

They were on her head.

But judging by the sheer terror on Marg's face, Jane knew, just knew that wasn't possible, someone in the village had stolen the apron.

The apron she had to win.

"Let me put ma batter in the fridge, get my driving shoes on and I'll drive us down," Jane said.

Marg slowly nodded.

Jane felt her stomach flip, churn and tighten, the apron being stolen scared her more than she wanted to admit.

***

After struggling to find her driving shoes, Jane had driven herself and Marg through the breathtaking village passing all the little stone houses and down to the massive green where the Festival was being held.

As Jane got out of her little red car (that her children called such an old lady car), she helped Marg out and watched her shuffle towards the massive green.

Jane had to admit it was beautiful.

On normal days the green was just a plain old

circle covered in grass, but it was days like this where it really came alive, and Jane just flat out loved it. She loved watching the large red tents that would fit almost a hundred people in stand strong in the gentle wind.

And as always the various shops from the bookstore to the green groceries to the optometrists were outside trying to get customers in the door, and like usual they were failing.

Jane turned her attention back to the tents and she really wanted to go inside and inspect all the competition, she could smell the most amazing chocolate chip, caramel and bacon cookies in the air that reminded her of her trips to America with her husband a few years ago.

People were shouting orders to the builders, talking and laughing as everyone prepared for the great opening of the Festival tomorrow and the cookies, cakes and everything else for the other competitions were safely inside the tents.

Jane wasn't exactly sure why all the food was being left in the tents overnight, but after living here all her life, she knew they would be perfectly safe.

"Come on Pet," Marg said as she shuffled towards the main red tent in the middle.

After walking over there (and helping Marg not fall over a few times), Jane's mouth dropped as she entered the tent. There were rows upon rows of tables lining the tent and they were all filled with the most amazing looking cakes, cookies and other magical creations Jane had ever seen. It was tough competition this year.

"Bourbon Creams!" Marg shouted.

As Marg hurried off to get something Jane's eyebrows rose when she realised Marg was getting another elderly lady who no one in the village knew her first name, everyone just called her Bourbon Creams because whenever you saw her, she would offer you a biscuit, a Bourbon Creams.

As if the world was determined to prove her right, Jane couldn't help but smile as she watched a tall hunched over lady walk over with Marg, and in her hand was a tub of freshly made Bourbon Creamss.

Normally Jane would at least try to say no, but considering someone had stolen the apron, she needed all the sugar and brain power she could get.

"Bourbon Jane?" the woman asked.

Jane nodded and took one. "Thanks,"

"Now Pet Bourbon Creams is the one who found ta apron was missing," Marg said.

Jane nodded. "Where was the apron kept?"

Bourbon Creams pointed Jane towards the large (slightly) terrifying) manakin in the middle of the tent that was now perfectly naked and even had some extra realistic things drawn on by the local kids as a joke.

"Did you see anyone? When was the apron last checked on?"

"Oh she quite good at this, isn't she Bourbon?"

Marg said. "I never would have thought to ask these,"

Jane finished off her biscuit and gestured for the lady to answer her.

"You know what Jane. I didn't see anything but the apron was still here last night when me, Bingo Lady and Sausage Lady were done,"

It was days like this that made Jane really understand why her children had left the village as soon as they could, the village was flat out strange and to be honest, as much as she loved it, it was just plain weird at times.

Jane forced herself to remember that the Bingo Lady was the little old lady who ran bingo at the town hall most nights, a great lady but utterly blind as a bat, so Jane doubted she could even see the apron let alone take it. Then Jane couldn't remember who was the Sausage Lady.

"The sausage Lady?" Jane asked.

"You know Pet? The butcher's wife,"

Jane could only smile at that. Mrs Hart wasn't the nicest of ladies on a good day, but as much as Jane wanted to get rid of her and she knew the village would be happier without her, Mrs Hart was far too pompous and arrogant to steal something that she would so easily win, at least that's what she always banged on about.

"What did the camera footage show from the local shops around the green?" Jane asked.

Marg and Bourbon Creams just looked at each other. "We didn't think of that Pet,"

Jane went back outside, breathed in the amazingly scented air and looked around for the best shop with the best angle to the front entrance of the main tent. Hopefully that shop would have a clear view of the person who entered it.

After a few moments she looked at the bookstore that was more or less right in front of the main entrance to the main tent, it was a bit far away so Jane seemed to remember the old man running the bookstore was a security nutter (or security conscious as her children kept reminding her).

Hopefully he would have the footage she needed.

Jane marched across the green towards the bookstore. She had to find the footage.

She had to find the apron.

***

As Jane sat down in a lumpy old chair with a massive ancient computer in front of her, Jane had to admit she hated the bookstore. She normally loved walking around, picking up the latest new book that was selling like crazy but the bookstore was useless at being modern when it came to tech.

But at least the wonderful smell of musty old books made the store feel more like a real bookstore that she had loved ever since she was a child.

"Here you go love," Mr Brooks said as he played the footage from last night for her.

Jane couldn't believe how bad the quality was, he was normally such a security nutter, she was expecting MI5 quality cameras, but even Jane's flip phone had a better camera on it than his security cameras.

But she managed to make out the footage of Bingo, Sausage and Bourbon Lady leaving around ten o'clock last night, then twenty minutes later another person ran across the green.

Well it looked like running but then she realised she had sped up the footage, so after she closed it, she realised someone was shuffling across the green towards the tent.

Jane immediately wondered if poor old Marg had really lost it and she had stolen the apron by mistake, but she knew what her best friend was like, she was old, forgetful and silly at times.

Yet she wouldn't forget something this important. It had to belong to someone else.

Then it twigged, Jane knew only one other person in the OAP village (as her children lovingly called it) that shuffled as badly as the person in the footage.

Someone she knew from school and someone who would always steal her things to get what they want.

Her old best friend.

"Thanks for that," Jane said to Mr Brooks as she placed a five pound note on the counter.

Jane quickly walked out of the store. She had to stop her former best friend and recover the apron.

Time was running out.

***

After picking up Marg and driving her up the

hills into the upper parts of the village, Jane parked her car outside a large stone house that was kept up perfectly, with its smooth walls, bright red door and the latest triple glazed windows.

Jane was not impressed. How dare her former best friend do this, she was going to get answers!

With Marg shuffling up behind her, Jane pounded on the red door.

After a few seconds, a tall lady (Mary Johnson) opened the door with her hands shaking, her hair looking wiry and her back hunched over.

"Where is it?" Jane asked with an edge.

Mary's eyes widened. "Where is what hun?"

"Don't play dumb with me Mary. I know you stole the Apron for the competition. Where is it?"

Mary went to shut the door but Jane forced her foot in front of it.

There was a thud.

"Help!" Mary shouted.

Jane slowly opened the door and there Mary was lying on the ground on her back and struggling to get up. Jane had forgotten how fragile Mary had become in recent years she wasn't surprised too much that simply stopping the door from shutting had knocked her over.

Marg went to shuffle past Jane but she placed her arm in front of Marg. Of course Jane felt bad but she really, really wanted this apron and to win the contest, she couldn't do any of that if Mary was hiding the apron.

"I'll help you up. Please tell me where the apron is?"

"Please," Mary said pleading.

"Come on Pet. Help her up," Marg said.

Jane shook her head. "I haven't spent years developing my cookie recipe for the apron to be stolen,"

"Fine," Mary said, showing her hands. "It's in my kitchen draws, top one on the left,"

Jane stared at her for a minute before helping her up, and Marg shuffled through the house into the kitchen.

"Are you okay? Need me to call 999?" Jane asked.

Mary pushed Jane away and stomped off upstairs.

A few seconds later, Marg shuffled back through holding the wonderful red, blue and gold apron. "Where's Mary? Did you kill her?"

Jane just smiled, took the apron and walked back out.

With little old Marg shuffling behind her.

***

The next day Jane couldn't believe how amazing she felt as the apron was placed over her in front of the entire village, everyone was clapping for her success and everyone loved her cookies.

The entire village smelt amazing with hints of cream, chocolate and many more amazing flavours danced on Jane's tongue and in her nose. It was truly the most amazing symphony of the senses, Jane wished this day would never end.

After Marg tied up the back of the apron, Jane waved and took a seat on a cold chair as the rest of the winners of the different contests were announced, Jane could only smile as her stomach flipped, filled with butterflies and kept getting excited.

Her mother would be so proud of her and Jane was proud of herself too, not only had she pleased her mother and solved a crime, but she had won the award she had always wanted.

And there was no better feeling than that.

So as soon as the rewards finished Jane knew she was going to socialise, celebrate and go home to phone her kids and tell them the most amazing news, and Jane just knew they would be over the moon for her.

And Jane couldn't wait for that. It was going to be the best ending to the best day she'd had for a long, long time.

STEALING AN ELECTION

Piper Burton really, really loved politics, international relations and so many more amazing political topics. Whether it was about the European Union or the amazing United Nations or even NATO, Piper loved them.

She honestly didn't know why she loved politics as much as she did, but there was no denying how passionate she got when she spoke about it. She truly believed that politics was a way for the masses to decide their future, regardless of how bad the politicians were.

In fact that was why Piper had been so desperate to go to the campaign headquarters of a Mr Jenson Jones who was currently running to be a Member of Parliament for Strood and Rochester in the South East of England.

Piper had always loved her hometown of Rochester. It was filled with history, great food and the little cobblestone high street was simply wonderful. Piper had loved going there with her friends as a teenager about a decade ago.

But now all of that was under threat.

For a woman who was meant to be very up-to-date on the latest political news, Piper still managed to surprise herself with not knowing about Mr Jenson Jones.

But as she stood in the cold wooden sports hall at a local school with the rest of his political team, Piper was seriously starting to wish she had never known him in the first place.

His politics was absolutely disgusting and now it made complete sense as to why no UK political party had accepted him. Especially considering all his policies were Anti-women, Anti-non-white-person and anti-gay.

And Piper was furious that even in the 21st century there were still dickheads like him about, that was why Piper wanted to... steer the election to a more politically suitable direction.

The massive wooden sports hall everyone was waiting in was where all the candidates were waiting for the official announcement to be made on who had won the election.

Piper had never seen so many people from different classes, races and political backgrounds in one place before. Granted Piper really wanted to try and cut the atmosphere with a knife, and it was still rather funny to watch everyone stick in their political groups.

Piper had managed to talk to some of the Red Party and other political parties that were more left-wing earlier in the evening, and Piper was grateful that they were more sane, friendly and actually wanted to do good in the local area.

The smell of everyone's sweat, perfume and aftershave combined into a completely awful smell that left the taste of salt on Piper's tongue, and now she seriously wished she didn't have to be here.

But this was where she needed to be to help steer democracy to where it needed to go, and Piper completely understood that this wasn't the more… politically correct way to deal with this far-far-right idiot, but Piper didn't exactly have many other options.

Especially since part of Jenson's campaign pledges was to kick out all gays, blacks and other non-whites from the constituency. Piper didn't want her best friends forced out of their homes, considering most of them and their families had lived in the UK since before world war two.

Compared to Jenson Jones who moved from America ten years ago. But apparently all migrants were awful people that needed to die.

Piper would happily see Jenson follow his own advice, but she never wanted people to suffer in politics.

"Miss Burton," a man about Piper's age said from behind her.

Piper turned around and grinned at the sight of

her old friend Ben who worked on the team for the Red Party representative in the election. Piper loved how he always had the most amazing blue eyes, skin and nails.

In all honesty Piper would have gone for him years ago quite easily if he wasn't gay.

"Hi Ben," Piper said.

"On a job again?" Ben asked, grinning.

Piper was thankful that Ben loved her like a sister. He was definitely the last person who would ever report her and considering her job would basically keep him and his friends safe, Piper was even more willing to bend the rules.

"I am an undercover journalist you know that," Piper said.

Ben just laughed. "Right,"

Then Ben pointed to her t-shirt, and Piper had to admit Jenson's uniform was terribly uncomfortable and it was bad enough being the only sane woman on the campaign. The other three women were conspiracy nuts, and Piper just wanted to slap some sense into them.

But Piper knew that the undercover journalist story wouldn't convince many people if she got caught.

"You're about the rigging then?" Ben asked.

Piper frowned and pretended to act cool. She had no idea about any rigging, sure she had lied to herself about the election being rigged so she felt okay about stealing this in favour of less extreme parties, but she didn't know that this could actually be true.

Ben took a few steps closer. "You don't know do you?"

Piper shook her head.

"Violet Hartley my candidate has some proof that Jenson has been buying people's votes. Each vote for him gets a person a thousand pounds wired through an offshore company,"

Piper gasped as that actually made a lot of sense. One of her jobs for the campaign was to manage the finances and she didn't understand it at the time, but tons of donations were going out of the country to an offshore company.

At least Piper now knew why.

Piper just looked at Ben and thankfully she knew that he would be up for anything if it kept him, his gay friends and other innocent people safe.

And stopping Jenson definitely would.

"I need a copy of that proof," Piper said quietly.

Ben shook his head. "That be hard Pi. I'll see what I can do. Where will you be?"

Piper just smiled. She wasn't going to tell him. But the only way to politically assassinate someone was to expose them so much that everyone in the entire country would hate them.

And that was a very, very fun thing to do.

Piper couldn't wait.

***

Piper was seriously not impressed with all her

friends in the local media. It turned out absolutely no one was interested in reporting or covering the story about Jenson rigging the elections. Not the TV studios, not the local papers, not even the three friends in National Radio that owned her some favours.

Piper was flat out not impressed in the slightest.

Her original plan had been to get the evidence, expose Jenson in front of everyone at the sports hall and get some of her media friends to film or record it. Then it wouldn't be hard for the national news stations to pick up the story.

That clearly wasn't happening.

And as much as Piper wanted to just get Ben to record it and post it up on social media, Piper had tried that before and its effect were so varied. Sometimes it worked, sometimes it didn't, sometimes it seriously didn't.

Piper couldn't risk that sort of variation with this job, she had to guarantee that Jenson would be politically assassinated. But thankfully Piper was always grateful for a massive flaw of the far-right, they always overreacted or went bananas if they discovered their leaders had betrayed them.

"Miss Burton," Jenson Jones said.

Piper turned slightly towards him as they both stood near the front stage in the sports hall and just smiled. She had to admit he was definitely a good looking man in his late thirties. He had smooth model-like skin, golden hair and the most seductive of smiles she had ever seen.

Granted that was really part of the problem, because that's one of the reasons why lots of women in the local area were voting for him. Because of apparently his looks were so amazing, and most women completely ignored his policies about *women should not leave the home unless accompanied by a man.*

Piper hated Jenson, but this wasn't the time. She subtly turned on the recorder app on her phone and Piper really hoped she could get some kind of admission of Jenson not believing in the far-far-right.

"Thank you Miss Burton for all your work," Jenson said.

"It was my pleasure Mr Jones,"

"It a shame you aren't going to be allowed out on the street from tomorrow," Jenson said stepping closer. "But you would be allowed out with me by your side,"

Piper wanted to punch him as she felt his wayward part extending against her ass as his horribly large muscular arms wrapped round her.

"You should tell your wife that," Piper said carefully.

Jenson laughed. "That submissive bitch is old. I much prefer stronger furious women,"

Piper smiled. That was almost perfect, that was so close to him basically admitting that women should be allowed to think for themselves and do other things besides housework.

She just needed a little more.

"Tell me Jenson," Piper said pushing herself against him, "would you like me to think up some special things for us to do?"

Jenson laughed in her ear. "Of course,"

Then Piper frowned as she realised she had accidentally given him exactly what his far-far-right mind wanted. Jenson hardcore believed that women were only good for childrearing, housework and sex. And Piper had just played into his sex ideology.

Piper tried to push away but Jenson wrapped his hands around her throat.

Piper watched the other members of his team and the staff of other right-wing political parties just stand there watching her. But there was something in their eyes, like this was her fault.

Jenson whispered seductively in Piper's ear. "Let's have a private conversation,"

Jenson started to push Piper away. She tried to protest but she couldn't do anything.

"Stop!" a woman shouted.

Piper headbutted Jenson and he released her.

Piper smiled when she saw ben standing next to a very tall elegantly dressed woman in all red just staring at Jenson.

"Violet I presume," Piper said, smiling.

Violet shook Piper's hand, but Piper subtly smiled when she felt something like a memory stick being passed into her hand. then Violet winked at her.

Ben quickly came over and hugged Piper then he led her away from Jenson. Piper was glad to be away from him.

He was scum that needed to pay.

Piper was determined to destroy him.

Especially now she had her proof of the rigging.

Piper just had to show it to the world.

***

Piper stood just behind a large red curtain that led out onto the hard wooden stage in the sports halls as she weighed up her options. She needed to prove to the world (or the country or these people at least) that Jenson was a criminal that rigged the election in his favour.

She just didn't know how to do it yet.

And considering the tension in the hall was even stronger now as well as more people had arrived and the announcement of the winner was getting closer and closer. Piper knew that time was running out.

Piper had seen proof on Ben's phone that he had sent it to various news agencies as a failsafe, but clearly none of them were covering the story yet.

Maybe that was the key though to all of this. The media was obviously the best instrument to commit political and character assassination and maybe the media just needed a bit more time.

The problem with elections was announcing there was fraud was always harder to do once the election result had been officially announced compared to before. So Piper really hoped that all she needed to do was delay the announcing of the election result until one of her media friends picked up the story.

That was a lot of hoping but Piper couldn't really see any more options. Unless she focused on assassinating Jenson's character in front of all of these people.

"Excuse me love," a man said.

Piper stepped to one side and watched two men carry a electrum, a small metal table and a laptop onto the stage. Piper watched them place the little laptop on the table and then Piper's eyes widened as she realised that the laptop was most properly connected to the hall's projector.

That was one of the great things about schools. Sometimes they had assemblies in the sports halls so there were always projectors in case a presentation needed to be given.

All Piper had to do was connect the memory stick to the laptop and project the evidence onto a wall so everyone could see it.

"Excuse me Miss," an elderly man said.

Piper looked at the man in his tight suit, shiny black shoes and his very official looking envelope. This was the man in charge of announcing the official election result.

"Mister," Piper said, grabbing him on the shoulder.

The man huffed. "What?"

Piper stepped closer to him. "I have some evidence that everyone here needs to see,"

The man shrugged. "And that affects me

because..."

Piper smiled. "Because I need you to let me borrow that laptop, the projector and you to delay the announcement,"

The man laughed. Hard. "Miss... whatever your name is. Per UK election law, I have to announce the results before 11 o'clock and I have already announced the result to Westminster,"

Piper rolled her eyes. "This vote is invalid, and I don't want you getting done for it,"

The man's eyes blinked. "What!"

"Two minutes. All I ask," Piper said.

The man nodded and looked like he was scared for what Piper was about to reveal.

Piper ran onto the stage, plugged in the memory stick and activated the projector. The entire sports hall fell silent as everyone probably believed she was going to reveal the results.

Violet and Ben glided through the crowd and stood in the front. Piper was really glad to see them.

After a second, tens upon tens of bank transfers showed up on the screen revealing how an offshore company owned by Jenson Jones had paid tons of people in this area a thousand pounds in the last two weeks.

No one reacted.

"Do you not know what this means?" Piper asked everyone.

Half the room nodded. Half the room laughed.

"It don't matter deary," Jenson said. "This is just

a left-wing fake created by women to scare us men. But we won't allow you bitches to oppress us anymore,"

Then Piper noticed a group of people with three massive cameras quietly walk in the back and Piper really hoped they started filming.

"You really think a woman could create this sort of fake?" Piper said. "I didn't think you believed women were smart enough,"

"Well you know what they say. Put enough dumb people together and something else pop up," Jenson said.

Piper just couldn't believe no one was reacting. She knew why Violet, Ben and the other Reds weren't reacting, because they knew she would do something. But it amazed Piper that the other right-wing people and some of the centralists didn't even react to this language.

Piper clicked the laptop a few times and zoomed in on the account and signatures.

"You signed these checks," Piper said. "You paid these voters for support. You got their vote for money, that isn't democracy,"

Jenson came up on stage. "That's a big word for such a little woman. But democracy is mob rule, we need strong leaders to lead us. And I will start my rule here,"

Piper subtly looked at the group at the back with the three massive cameras and judging by the concerned looks on their faces with some a very small smiles too. Piper was sure they were news reporters and they had definitely recorded it.

And since that dickhead Jenson was never going to confess directly. Piper just wanted the entire election to be made a laughing stock off, and that would happen as soon as everyone found out that Jenson had won.

"Go ahead," Piper said to the man with the tight suit, black shoes and envelope.

The man raced up on the stage and ripped open the envelope.

"And the winner is Violet Hartley. She is the new MP for Strood and Rochester representing the Red Party Parliamentary Party," he said.

Piper just smiled.

That was pleasantly unexpected and that would actually help her a damn sight more with finishing off Jenson.

***

Piper absolutely loved reading all the inventive, fascinating and amazing headlines that filled the media and newspapers the next day. Piper hadn't been expecting too much more than the normal announcement of who won the election.

But it turned out Piper exposing the truth behind Jenson's criminal activity that had had a much, much larger impact than she ever believed possible.

All the papers and news outlets were leading with the same basic story that focused on how stupid Jenson and his far-right policies were. And how for his criminal activity, it just went to prove that no one wanted the far-right in power.

It still bugged Piper more than she wanted to admit that Jenson had gotten 25% of the vote and those were clearly his true supporters, but she supposed there was actually a bit of hope in all this.

If this election had proved anything to Piper, it was no matter how much hate, chaos and intolerance the far-right tried to spread throughout society. There would always be those who realised that hate was never the answer to other so-called problems, and Piper really found that hopeful.

So as she stood in the wooden sports halls that was perfectly tidy, clean and she was the only person in there, Piper was really looking forward to the future. Because this election had proved that there was a chance that hate could be beaten.

And it turned out without Piper, the media never would have created the headlines and character and political assassination that the country wanted. Jenson was finished, and he was thankfully being arrested and charged for electoral fraud and he was never ever allowed to run for parliament again.

Piper just smiled at that as she started to walk out of the sports hall, all she could do was feel very, very proud of what she had helped to achieve last night.

Because she had come here wanting to steal an election and defeat Jenson.

But she had done one better, she had made sure the right leader was elected, and she had all but annihilated Jenson once and for all, so him and his ideas and policies could never hurt an innocent person again.

And that made her feel utterly amazing.

AUTHOR OF BETTIE ENGLISH PRIVATE EYE MYSTERIES
CONNOR WHITELEY

THE BIG FIVE WHOOPEE MOMENTS
A MYSTERY CRIME SHORT STORY

THE BIG FIVE WHOOPEE MOMENTS

My name is Hunter Carter, I'm 80 years old and I can thankfully say I had a very full life filled with a wonderful husband, job and five big whoopee moments.

Until I lost it all, in a way

***

My first big whoopee moment had to be when I was about ten years old on Christmas Eve. My wonderful daddy had just died and the house felt really, really terrible.

But as I stood on the cold wooden floor at the very top of the stairs, I knew my mummy was going to make Christmas magical, even without daddy. I knew all of her amazing cooking going on. She was baking my favourite nutmeg cookies and other hints of cinnamon, mixed spices and oranges filled the air.

Just at that moment I knew Christmas was going to be amazing, and I knew me and mummy would help each other through the thing I would later know was called heartbreak.

I really loved my daddy. He always supported me, loved me and made sure I had the best possible childhood, so I knew if I was ever going to have children of me own. I would try and be like my daddy.

The gentle sounds of Christmas songs, mummy laughing and being happy echoed through the entire house.

Then I realised that she had to be talking to Santa and he was making her laugh.

My smile just grew and grew and grew at the idea of having Santa in *my* house, delivering my presents and he was even making time to check on my mummy after daddy died.

Santa was such an amazing guy and even though he had all the presents to deliver he was still making us feel special, loved and cared for. Or maybe something else was going on.

Maybe daddy was Santa?

Maybe when mummy said daddy wasn't going home anymore because him and his car went up to the big scrapyard in the sky. He had traded in his car for a sleigh and he was helping Santa.

That was amazing! My daddy was Santa!

Whoopee!

***

My next whoopee was at the amazing age of sixteen, and after a massive fight at home with mother and her dick head of a boyfriend, who was the man making her laugh on Christmas Eve when I was ten. I just wanted to drive off and never come home.

Well, that plan had lasted exactly ten minutes before I decided to call a special friend from school.

I was furious with mum letting her idiot boyfriend treat me like I was nothing, a criminal for being gay and like I was an absolute failure that I just wanted to do something that idiot would deem unforgivable.

So I called up a great looking guy from school who was Captain of the Football team, really smart and so fit. A guy called Harry Rodden.

And as I finished driving up to a great secluded spot in the woods. I just couldn't believe I was in the car with such a great sexy guy with his six-foot-six body with slight muscles, blond hair and such a cute face that I just wanted to kiss all night (and planned to).

I parked the car and made sure the lights were off then Harry grabbed my head and we made out. His soft lips tasted so amazing and he had clearly done this before.

As we continued kissing, he started to run his hands up my body, unbuttoning my shirt and within minutes we were both basically naked making out in my car.

And it felt great!

Then he started to run his fingers up my leg, he grabbed my balls and started massaging them.

Needlessly to say it was only a few minutes later that I shouted something we both loved.

"Whoopee!"

***

About ten very short years later, me and sexy gorgeous Harry were married and living together. I had always loved our massive house with four bedrooms, a large garden that led out into a little river and our kitchen was all state of the art.

I leant against the wonderfully smooth marble kitchen island that had warmed up tons because the amazing sunlight. I seductively stared at how amazing Harry looked with his model-like looks, longish blond hair and just flat out gorgeous lips. I really had been so lucky to have him in my life, and even though we had been married for a few years, we were still passionately in love with each other.

Harry kept on reading whatever magazine he was, and he would occasionally look at me and blew me a kiss.

The kitchen still smelt sensational of bacon, eggs and salmon from the very posh lunch I had cooked us earlier to celebrate each other. There was no reason, it wasn't his or mine birthday or any special occasion for that matter.

I just wanted him to know I loved him, and I definitely knew that he loved me.

The sound of some letters falling through the letterbox made me and Harry both smile at each other, and Harry went to look at the letters. Whilst I stared at his amazingly fit ass as he went.

We were both really hoping it was a letter for me from the university telling me I had passed my PhD and was now a doctor of clinical psychology (just think mental health), and that would finally allow me to start helping people, improving lives and just do what I always wanted to do.

Harry came back into the kitchen with a massive smile on his face and he held out a letter towards me.

I couldn't help but smile as I took the letter, opened it and found out that I had passed with top marks. And to my utter surprise there was also a letter of recommendation from the head of my university programme.

I had no idea I had impressed him that much, but judging by the glowing letter he gave me. He was clearly impressed and now the world really was my oyster.

"Whoopee!" I shouted as I wrapped my arms round Harry and kissed that sexy perfect man hard.

***

It had been two amazing decades since I became a doctor and I was loving my life. I had thankfully worked with some of the most amazing doctors in the UK, gotten to help so many clients that needed to improve their lives and I was thankfully able to open my own clinic recently.

As I sat at my very expensive leather desk chair with my great oak desk in front of me and a bunch of client folders laid out. I just had to look up from my work and I just smiled.

I really had the best life. I could work my own hours, pay myself whatever I wanted and thankfully life was so perfect.

Well. Except from home, and that was really the reason why I opened this clinic in the first place. Harry had become a major (and I do mean major) business person in the past few decades so he was constantly flying around the world, meaning other businessmen and fucking them too.

All whilst I had been left at home alone and forced to entertain myself, so I had opened this clinic and thankfully it used up tons of my time.

My office was normally a hive of activity but considering it was 6 pm in the evening. I was alone and had some jazz music playing softly in the background and some vanilla scented candles burned slowly in the background.

All I had to do was finish up this paperwork on the folders, and then I could call in my… very special fun.

And since Harry was travelling around the world doing every man that moved, I had tried to resist the urge for about a decade to just copy him. But I had a major problem when I opened this clinic.

I had hired a very young, attractive and adorable secretary.

When I hired Luca he was 20 years old and he worked part-time as a model for an underwear company, but I suspected judging by the amount of tailored suits he wore to work that they also did some suits, shirts and trousers on the side.

During the first month of Luca working here, I hadn't given him much thought. Sure, he was fit as anything, had a stunning face and had the most perfect ass I had ever seen. But I never ever planned to do something about that slight attraction.

All until one late night we had both been working together on modernising our filing system, and he just made a move. And I was powerless to stop him.

The sound of my office door quietly open made me smile as I knew exactly who it was, and as much as I wanted to finish up this paperwork, I just had to enjoy the possible view too.

So I looked up at the door, but Luca was standing right in front of my desk in nothing but a jockstrap and damn he looked good.

"Like what you see," Luca asked.

I just nodded. "Whoopee,"

***

My final whoopee moment was a lot greater in some ways but deadly in others.

It was Christmas Eve and I had just finished giving Luca an amazing Christmas present that he utterly loved, groaned and had a few of his own whoopees. And when I opened the door to my massive house the air smelt amazing with hints of nutmeg, mixed spices and oranges just like my mummy used to make.

I was so glad that Harry had come home and he had actually decided to have an interest in me, our marriage and I honestly believed he wanted to make sure things worked out.

So I went through to our massive kitchen and I watched Harry place a freshly baked tray of amazing dark brown sugar cookies on a wire track on our kitchen island.

And I just stared him as I realised he was baking naked, and wow… him working away so much and eating at some of the world's finest restaurants really hadn't damaged his figure in the slightest.

Even after all these years he still looked just as stunning as he did all those years ago in my car at age 16.

This was definitely an amazing whoopee moment.

Harry came over to me, kissed me on the lips and I seriously loved the taste of his sexy soft lips against mine.

"Have one babe," he said, pointing to the wonderfully smelling cookies, and I did.

The cookie was the best I had ever tasted and there was such a great taste of bitter almonds that really-

I started coughing.

I loosened my tie.

Nothing helped.

I collapsed to the ground.

Harry stomped on my chest.

"You're mine you bitch. You're my property. You'll never have sex again," Harry said.

As my world went black and I presumed all life drained from my body, all I could think was how great of a whoopee moment this could have been.

***

I was completely surprised when I opened my eyes and found myself in a warm hospital bed with horribly thin blue sheets, various pieces of equipment around me and not a window in sight. I couldn't believe I had been so lucky.

Sure the hospital room stunk of ammonia with hints of death, rot and sickness barely covered by it. I was just glad to be alive.

"Hunter Carter," a deep voice said.

I looked towards the door and saw a very overweight but friendly looking cop standing there smiling. He gestured if he could come in and I nodded.

"You gave us quite the scare," he said. "You should be glad that your boy toy Luca went to your house after he tried to call you twice,"

For some reason I just smiled, sure there was 15 years between me and Luca, but he was a great man. And I think I did honestly care about him, so no, he was never a boy toy. He was someone I actually did care about.

And he clearly cared about me if he had called the cops and tried to save me.

"The cookies and the bitter almonds?" I asked.

The cop just nodded. "Your husband really wanted you dead, but he wasn't very good at getting the dosage right. Don't worry Harry Rodden has been arrested and charged for the attempted murder,"

I just nodded. That was great news.

"And it turned out your husband wasn't only abusing you," the cop said. "He had men under his control all over the world on his so-called business trips. But you were the only one who he ever tried to kill,"

I sort of felt like the cop was trying to flatter me, but I only felt lucky to be alive.

"What day is it?" I asked.

The cop laughed. "26th December. Boxing Day Mr Carter, and someone has spent all Christmas here waiting for you,"

I had no clue who it was, but as an extremely handsome face popped round the door. I just stared at how amazingly cute Luca was in his tight jeans, white shirt and black shoes. He really did look like a model, but he was more than that.

From what Luca had told me guys just saw him for his looks, wayward parts and his age. But he also mentioned that I was the first person ever to see past all that, and I had actually gotten to know the real Luca.

The sweet man that was one of the sweetest people I had ever met.

And as he came into my hospital room and hugged me, I loved the sensational feeling of love, chemistry and respect flow between us.

So whatever happened now after the New Year, I was really looking forward to having this great man next to me.

And a great man that completed me, loved me and made me feel the best I had ever been since I was 16.

***

Not bad for a man who only had Five Big Whoopees Moments in his life, some people sadly don't get any.

TO DIE IN SERVICE

This was the day Mathew died.

Detective Sergeant Mathew Horne was not your sort of everyday senior cop that just loved to off-load work onto junior officers or other people below him. Most DSs loved doing that because it gave them more time to do paperwork, lunch with the higher-ups or simply because it made their lives easier.

Instead Mathew just loved investigating, solving crimes and helping people. Ever since he had been a teenager and read his first mystery book, watched his first police TV drama and solved who stole his lunch money, he had wanted to become a real cop.

And as he sat at his very comfortable desk in his own private office that was very well hidden at the back at the police station, he felt damn well proud to be a cop.

Sure there were plenty of drawbacks. Like the bad pay, rubbish coffee and the occasional injury on the job, but Mathew still wouldn't have it any other way.

Mathew enjoyed the smell of a junior officer's perfume that was quite the looker too, but Mathew still made sure to tell off any higher-ups or anyone else for that matter who caused her problems.

That alone had caused Mathew to be suspended once or twice (or maybe even three times) but Mathew was never going to allow any cops to sexually harass someone, no matter how great they looked.

The smell of someone's sausage, bacon and egg lunch from out in the bullpen must have been spiced with something strong as Mathew could smell it from here. Leaving a wonderful spicy taste on his tongue.

He needed to get some tacos later on that was for sure.

The sounds of people talking, filling in reports and on the phone echoed all around the station, and even with the thick office walls Mathew could still make out a lot of what was said.

But Mathew really didn't mind that.

One of his first concerns about being a DS had been about missing the action and not feeling like he was a part of the other cops, but thankfully with all the sounds he didn't feel like that in the slightest.

And he loved it.

A loud knock at the door made Mathew look up and he instantly smiled as the junior officer Luna Winter with the amazing smelling perfume walked into Mathew's office.

She was still easily two metres from him and

Mathew had to force himself not to choke on the strong flowery perfume of hers.

Mathew was slightly tempted to tell Luna that she needed to start putting on less, but with her long ginger hair, innocent blue eyes and amazing figure. He just couldn't bring himself to be even slightly negative towards her.

She was great.

"Serg," Luna said smiling.

"Officer," Mathew said, "is there a problem?"

Luna looked at the door and she was presumably making sure it was closed. That made Mathew concerned, he had never seen another officer do that and give him good news.

"Sir," Luna said, "I think we have a cop on the take here,"

Mathew didn't know how to react to such a thing. He had worked with the vast majority of the officers here and Mathew knew them so well. It was impossible to imagine any of them were working for the criminals and taking pay-offs.

"Have you taken this to the higher-ups?" Mathew asked.

Luna frowned. "You think they would believe me?"

Mathew almost pointed out that he didn't believe her exactly, but he wanted to see where this was going and if there was any proof then Mathew knew he sadly had to deal with it.

"I guess not. What proof have you got?"

Luna looked around again and took out her phone. She swiped away at it and then showed Mathew something.

It took him a few moments to realise he was looking at various bank account records that showed thousands of pounds being sent to a recurring account every month like clockwork.

"Who are these accounts?" Mathew asked.

Luna took a deep breath. "These are the bank accounts sieged in a drug raid yesterday. I was sent to help process the scene and secure it,"

Mathew wasn't exactly sure he believed her about processing it, but he knew that some junior officers were just told that so they got there quicker. Hell, he had used that lie a few times because some officers were just so slow unless it was something that they deemed *exciting*.

"And you think this other mystery is linked to the police?" Mathew asked.

Luna slowly nodded. "You're the smartest man we know in the entire station. If you can't work it out then no one can,"

Mathew smiled. "You didn't answer my question,"

"Sorry Serg. Yea I ran the account and it came back to a Shell Company called Tyson Limited. It's a fake company with no employees, trading accounts or money it seems,"

"But the transfers?" Mathew asked.

Luna nodded. "Exactly. The funds are

immediately withdrawn and the money goes,"

Mathew stood up and paced around the officer for a few moments.

"The police connections?" he asked.

Luna took in a long deep breath. "Tyson is the surname of our boss you remember. The Police Captain and he has been buying a lot of things lately,"

Mathew just shook his head. There was no way Police Captain Finley Tyson would be involved in criminal activity, he was a great man. A very principled and hard line man when it came to crime, but she did have a point.

It was only yesterday that Mathew had seen the Captain arrive at the station in his brand new BMW, his wife had just bought a Land Rover and Mathew had noticed the Captain wearing an expensive 24 carat gold watch.

Something was dodgy about that.

Mathew just looked at Luna. If she was right then this was going to be extremely hard to prove and extremely serious. If Mathew made even a small mistake then his entire career would be over.

That was too big a risk, so Mathew wanted to run three tests first.

Mathew went back to his desk and took out his phone and subtly checked the Captain's bank accounts. Even that would get him fired and technically without a warrant none of this would be useful.

The bank accounts were normal and showed the

pay outs for the new cars. But it didn't show how the Captain got the money in the first place.

Then Mathew checked the Company Register to see who owned Tyson Limited, and a Mr Finley Tyson did. The exact same Finley Tyson that was the Police Captain.

Mathew just looked at Luna. She smiled.

Mathew had to be careful here.

He had to stop the Police Captain.

Or risk his career ending.

And letting a corrupt cop walk free.

***

The third test was simple enough.

Mathew really didn't want to have to open an official investigation because he would definitely be shut down, fired and blacklisted, so he would never be able to be a cop again.

And considering all the run-ins Mathew had had with those people that pretended to be professional, but they were only Private Investigators. Mathew was determined to never become one of those people.

Instead Mathew wanted to test his theory by going directly to the source itself, he wanted to talk to Captain Finley in person without Luna, any other cops or anyone else for that matter. He needed to see if Luna was right.

As Mathew walked into Finley's large square office that was tastelessly decorated in horrible brown tones, blood red rugs and a massive oak desk in the middle that looked like it was about to collapse at any moment, Mathew was starting to see why Finley might be corrupt.

"Detective Sergeant," Finley said with a massive smile.

Mathew smiled at Finley who sat at his desk smiling and doing paperwork, and Mathew feared that his seat would collapse at any moment.

It was certainly bending enough.

Mathew didn't mind that Finley was definitely a larger man but now he was starting to wonder if he was corrupt because he had unofficially been demoted to desk duty.

Mathew seriously doubted Finley was fit enough to chase down any criminals, even as a Police Captain they normally went out and around every so often to meet and greet the members of the public, and do other community work.

But maybe Finley had a different reason for why he was corrupt. If he was at all.

When he had overheard Internal Affairs talk about corruption, it always tended to stem from the police not being paid properly for all the hard work they did, and Mathew did partly agree. But he loved this job anyway, so he would understand if the Captain felt the need to create other income streams for himself.

At least that way he would be able to buy himself a proper desk and get some half-good decoration.

Mathew really hated those horrible carpets and brown tones. They were just flat ridiculous.

Mathew made sure the office door was closed and then he leant over Finley's desk and spoke very quietly to him.

"Sir," he said. "I have had something bought to my attention and it's... a delicate topic,"

Finley just frowned. "Seriously DS Horne. Did Internal Affairs really get you to question me?"

Mathew's eyebrows rose. He had no clue Finley was being investigated, and that was extremely serious. Internal Affairs never really got involved unless they had some kind of evidence.

As much as Mathew wanted to leave and abandon this investigation for IA to sort out, he just wanted to find out what the hell was going on.

"What do they have on you?" Mathew asked.

Finley just stared at Mathew for a moment. "You aren't working for them,"

Mathew shook his head. "Sir, I respect the hell out of you, but why is IA investigating?"

Finley huffed. "Fine then Matt. It's because of my new cars, watch and some home improvements I did,"

Mathew nodded. He had heard through the grapevine that the Captain had redone his house and added a loft conversion so his grandkids had their own special place to play when they came over. It actually sounded like a great idea.

"Where did the money come from?" Mathew asked.

Finley looked around. "My wife. Her uncle died a

few years ago and there was a clause in the Trust Fund he left her, if she didn't get into legal trouble for the next five years then she could get the cash. That's where the money came from,"

Mathew seriously wanted to ask about his wife because he had met her a few times, and she was such a great woman. Mathew couldn't believe she was criminally inclined, but maybe this uncle was just paranoid or something.

Mathew didn't really want to ask.

"Does IA know?" Mathew asked.

Finley nodded. "I literally just finished phoning them. They're investigating it now, but they wanted to know about a corrupt officer in the department,"

Mathew folded his arms and paced around the office for twice.

"Who told you about the IA suspicions?" Finley asked.

Mathew just stopped. Then he very quickly realised that IA would never tell anyone else about their investigation unless they needed to as a last resort. There was no way Luna should have known about the investigation unless-

"Officer Luna," Mathew said slowly.

Finley stood up and Mathew was tempted to hold on to the walls as the entire office shook with each of Finley's steps.

"She was one of IA's suspects. They think she was secretly stealing drugs, money and other things from crime scenes," Finley said.

Mathew wanted to punch a wall so badly. That sexy woman had manipulated him so easily and it made perfect sense really.

She had even told him she wanted to see how smart he was, and if he was smart enough to basically catch her.

Mathew had to find her.

Capture her.

And bring her to justice.

***

Mathew got out of his little black car in an underground car park where not a single other car was located, he really hated these sorts of places.

The car park was perfectly dark with a few lights failing to illuminate much of anything. Mathew had texted Luna to meet him here and that he had massive news to tell her about the investigation.

The smell of rot, urine and a dead rat filled the air and Mathew really hoped it wouldn't take her long to get here.

A few moments later Mathew saw a large red mini drive into the car park and it was heading straight for him.

It sped up.

Mathew jumped out the way.

The car smashed into a concrete wall.

Mathew carefully walked over and saw Luna's dead body at the wheel, and Mathew was shocked to see all her beauty was gone.

Then Mathew noticed the massive slash across

her throat and that scared him. Everything had pointed towards her being the corrupt cop, but someone had killed her. But why?

Mathew couldn't understand why someone would want to kill such a kind, beautiful woman that only wanted to find a corrupt cop.

"She should have minded her own business," Finley said from behind him.

Mathew turned around and saw Finley standing there with a massive kitchen knife dripping warm fresh blood onto the ground. Mathew wanted to run, scream and call for help, but clearly that wasn't going to work.

"The Trust Fund was fake" Mathew said.

Finley nodded. "Don't worry DS Horne. I told IA about your scheme with your secret girlfriend, and when she wanted to come clean you killed her,"

Mathew just shook his head. "And what you tried to stop me and I attacked you and you killed me in self-defence?"

"Of course," Finley said.

"Why?" Mathew asked.

Finley laughed. "Because you saw my office. It's a shithole and my life is a pile of shit while the criminals we capture are living in houses I could never afford, they have more women I could ever dream of and so much more,"

Mathew just had to laugh at how stupid Finley was being, being a cop was never about the money, the benefits and all that rubbish. Being a cop was about serving and protecting the amazing people in their community.

Mathew looked behind Finley and tried to decide if he was quick enough to run.

Finley rammed the knife into his stomach.

Crippling pain rushed through Mathew.

Mathew grabbed the knife.

Finley looked concerned.

Mathew headbutted Finley.

The fat bastard fell back.

Mathew held onto the knife.

He didn't let go.

Finley released the knife.

He landed on the floor.

Mathew ripped out the knife.

Thrusted it into Finley's neck.

Mathew just about managed to pull the knife out before his own wounds started to become too much to bear, and the worse crippling pain Mathew had ever experienced claimed him.

As Mathew fell to the ground he knew that his life had been great, helpful and he really had done his best to be a cop. Mathew had loved solving crimes, helping people and making people believe that the police really was a force for good.

Because it was.

And whilst people might stupidly believe he was a corrupt cop, Mathew just knew that Internal Affairs, his cop friends and his family would quickly see through the lies of Finley.

Everyone would know he had died in service protecting the police, stopping a bad man walk free and really living up to the values of the police.

And as the last of his life drained away from him, Mathew couldn't deny that dying in service to a cause he loved made him feel amazing.

BOOK THIEF

Jane Smith, amateur sleuth, had always loved reading ever since she was a little girl, over 60 years ago, she loved being transported to new worlds to make new friends and go on exciting new adventures.

So when her best friend Marg had told her about a stolen book in their quiet little village in the south of England, Jane had to go and investigate, or at least have a nose around (or be a pain in the backside as her children lovingly said).

Jane stood outside a massive stone cottage in the centre of the little village and she loved it. Unlike her small stone cottage, this one was made from stunning white stone that reflected the sunlight perfectly, making the cottage seem a lot more impressive than it actually was.

It reminded Jane of when her and her husband had moved to the village over fifty years ago and had looked at a similar cottage, he had always said it was too expensive and had far, far, far too many "modern" features that took away from its natural beauty.

Jane could only smile at his words now, she wished he was still around to see the cottage now.

Jane ran her fingers across the cold blue wooden door as she prepared herself to knock, she could see the gentle blowing of the wind rustling the flowers behind her, but the sounds of laughing, moaning and shouting was clear enough behind the door.

Jane didn't know what was going on but she could hear one of the voices clearly enough. The cottage belonged to a Mrs Willy Anne, Jane had never liked her, she thought of herself as god's gift to mankind and she make sure people knew it.

As Jane smelt the wonderful hints of chocolate, butter and biscuits in the air, Jane had to smile as she knew who was here instantly. A woman who everyone called Bourbon Creams was inside and no doubt she had a tub of Bourbon Creams in her hands ready to offer anyone a biscuit or two, even if they didn't want it.

Jane took in a deep chocolatey breath and knocked on the door three times.

But she wasn't expecting to hear silence then a strange shuffling sound as if someone or something was being moved over to the door to answer it.

When the door opened, Jane instantly smiled as her best friend Marg stared at her, wearing a rather beautiful pink hat, summer dress and even some red nail polish. For Marg, that was scandalous.

Jane gave Marg a quick hug and walked into the large cottage to be greeted with a large brown room with bookshelves lining the outside of it. There were hundreds of first editions there, Jane didn't know how much it was all worth but it must have been hundreds of thousands.

She could understand why someone wanted to steal from it.

Yet the strange thing was Jane couldn't see a single gap in all the shelves so the stolen book clearly wasn't taken from down here, as far as Jane could see.

"Bourbon?" a tall elegant woman said holding out a tub of freshly made Bourbon Creams.

"No thank you," Jane said, smiling.

"What is *that* woman doing here?"

As soon as Jane heard her she knew who the speaker was, it was Willy, the arrogant, annoying person herself. Jane wondered whether or not she should just leave, but she really, really wanted to know more about this stolen book.

Willy walked over to Jane and stopped right in front of her. Jane almost gagged at all her horrible perfume and Willy was wearing far too much makeup for being indoors.

But Jane wouldn't have been surprised if her first reaction to finding the book had been stolen, was to put on more makeup.

"Mrs Jane Smith," she said holding out her hand.

"*I* do not shake the hands of *you* people,"

Jane took a deep breath and gestured for

Bourbon Creams to give her one. She was definitely going to need the sugar.

Marg stood next to Jane. "Come on Willy, she here to help ya,"

Willy rolled her eyes. "If you are not going to speak the Queen's English, then please leave,"

Jane laughed. "I take it the police haven't been?"

"Why would I invite *those* people into my home? I do not want the theft to become a national scandal,"

Jane forced herself not to laugh, she couldn't believe the arrogance of this woman, and quite frankly the mystery of the stolen book was the only thing keeping her.

Marg waved Willy away and turned to Jane. "Hi Pet, I need ya help,"

Jane smiled. "Sure thing Marg. What you need? What happened?"

"Oh pet, it was a terrible thing. I loaned Willy bumface over there, one of my first editions, my hubby loved it before he died,"

Jane took another deep breath, she knew how much Marg had loved her husband, so it was amazing that Marg was still able to breathe and talk without crying about the theft.

She had to help her.

"I lent it to bumface yesterday. I came to pick it up today and she had lost it Pet," Marg said.

Jane just glared at Willy.

"It is not my fault, that the book is lost," she said.

Jane went over to her and went very close to her ear. "You will help me find my friend's book, or I will leak it to the newspapers, the BBC and every single little blog in this area,"

Willy's eyes widened in horror. Jane smiled as that was exactly the reaction she wanted.

"Of course I would love to help you Marg," Willy said, "to find your book. I will give you whatever you need, and cover your insurance,"

Jane cocked her head at that point. Clearly Willy wasn't very knowledgeable about her neighbours, everyone knew that normal people didn't have top notch insurance for first editions and other priceless objects, so why would she assume that?

"You don't have insurance?" Jane asked.

"Yes Pet, hubby got it a week before he died,"

Jane's eyebrows rose. That alone was strange, Jane had been best friends with Marg for close to 50 years and she had no idea she had a first edition and that it was insured. So how did Willy know?

Jane went very close to Marg. "How did Will know? Did you tell her?"

"Yea Pet. Showed her the insurance paperwork last night,"

"Are you insured for theft?" Jane asked.

Marg shuffled around for a few moments before looking back at Jane. "I think so Pet,"

Bourbon Creams went round offering everyone another biscuit. Jane declined and was about to open her mouth when she closed it.

She wanted to ask Willy if she had stolen it because Marg would get the money from the insurance company, and then Willy could sell it and pocket the money for herself. But she doubted Willy would just admit it so easily.

Jane needed to find out about the finances of Willy Anne to see if she had motive.

"You know Willy, I have always wanted to see the view from the master bedroom, my husband before he died always regretted never seeing these massive cottages,"

Willy rolled her eyes. "Well that is *your* problem,"

Jane really forced herself not to laugh. "But please Willy, I would love to see the upstairs. My husband would probably haunt you if you said no,"

To Jane's surprise, Willy's face went ghostly white and her hands even started shaking. Jane gently elbowed Marg in the arm.

"Oh yes Willy Pet, my husband haunted one of my kids for years until she told me the truth about my necklace. My husband was nasty about that sort of thing,"

Jane smiled.

"My husband once even tried to crash my daughter's car. That was bad of him. If he does that to family Pet, then what would he do to you?" Marg said.

Willy fainted.

Bourbon Creams went to take out her phone but didn't.

Jane just looked at her. "You'll be okay with what we want to do right?"

Bourbon Creams just nodded. "Bumface, stole ma Custard Cream recipe years ago. I gonna find it,"

"Good luck," Jane said.

As Bourbon Creams walked off into the cottage, Jane looked around for another door of some kind but couldn't see anything. All the walls were just bookcases.

"What ya looking for Pet?"

"A door? The Stairs?" Jane asked.

Marg shuffled over to a bookcase on the far wall and pulled over a large bible. The sound of clicking filled the air and then Jane noticed a long wooden staircase was coming down from the ceiling.

As Marg started to shuffle up the stairs, Jane wondered about moving Willy into a comfortable position, but she was breathing so she was fine.

Jane went up the stairs.

When her and Marg got to the top, Jane was stunned at the massive hallway staring back at her, there were tens of different rooms that the finances could be in.

Marg started shuffling down the hallway like she knew where she was going.

"Where you going Marg?"

"Come on Pet, bumface took me to the office last night,"

Jane nodded and followed her down the hallway. She couldn't believe how many bedrooms, storage rooms and other empty rooms were in the cottage. Jane had no idea the cottage went back this far.

"Why do you call her bumface?" Jane asked.

Marg just shrugged. "Cos she annoying Pet,"

Jane couldn't argue there. After a few more moments, Marg turned into a little brown room and Jane followed.

The sound of musty old books filled the air and Jane gagged. It smelt disgusting, and there were other awful hints of old coffee, sandwiches and even peanut butter. Jane really didn't want to be in here.

After Jane forced her attention away from the smell, she focused on all the rows upon rows of first editions that covered each of the walls and a massive desk was in the middle.

Jane was hardly impressed with all the paper on the desk but at least it was in some kind of order. She went over it and started to look through it.

Marg searched the books. "Ya know Pet, we quite good at these detective lark,"

"Yea we are," Jane said as she picked up some documents about rare booksellers.

"Stuff must be worth a fortune Pet," Marg said as she took out an ancient red leather book but grunted.

Jane looked up. "What's wrong?"

"It feels wrong Pet," Marg said as she walked over to Jane and opened the book.

Jane's mouth dropped as the book fell apart, not because it was ancient, but because it was fake. It was nothing more than a piece of cardboard with a leather cover on top.

Marg went over and started opening more and more and more books. They were all fake.

"So she doesn't have a rare book collection?"

"Na pet,"

"Then…" Jane said as she picked up the leather book cover.

As Jane ran her fingers in-between the leather cover and focused on its texture, feeling and even the smell, Jane sort of remembered something her husband mentioned once about how to tell if the leather is real.

The book covers were definitely real, but the insides weren't.

Jane couldn't understand that. Why keep the real covers, but destroy, sell or do something with the actual books themselves?

"I see *you* people have found my secret?"

Jane dropped the cover and stared at Willy.

She was holding a knife. Jane rushed over to Marg and forced herself in-between her friend and the knife.

"Why?" Jane asked, knowing she needed to think about this quickly.

Willy shook her head. Waving the knife around.

"Come on bumface, tell us the truth!"

Willy pointed the knife at Jane's chest.

"Not helpful Marg," Jane said.

"Not trying be helpful Pet,"

"Silence! I need to think!" Willy said walking about.

Jane looked at the desk. Maybe she could use the papers on it.

"Where's my book bumface?"

Willy flew over.

Jane forced Marg back.

The knife pressed against her chest.

"Tell your friend to shut up!" Willy shouted.

Jane shook her head. No one threatened her best friend.

"You! Shut up!" Jane said.

Willy swung the knife.

Jane jumped back.

Willy screamed.

Charging at Jane.

Pushing Jane against the wall.

Willy thrust the knife.

Jane grabbed it.

Willy was strong.

Too strong.

The blade got closer to Jane's throat.

Marg rushed behind the desk.

She whacked the papers.

They flew everywhere.

Willy was blind.

Jane kicked her.

Willy stumbled.

Jane kicked her.

Willy hissed.

Marg shuffled over.

Punching Willy in the head.

Willy fell to the ground.

Dropping the knife.

Jane picked it up.

It was over.

"Bourbon Creams anyone?" the woman asked as she stood in the doorway.

***

Jane stood outside in front of the awful large cottage as she watched the police drive off with Willy Anne in the back seat.

As Jane crunched on a Bourbon Creams, letting the wonderful chocolatey creamy flavours explode on her tongue, she definitely realised her husband had been right the entire time. These large stone cottages were horrible and she was glad they had never got one.

Marg shuffled outside and stood next to Jane holding a stunning fully- illustrated first edition of a famous book, Jane couldn't help but smile.

She might not have found it herself, but Jane still liked to think she had helped her best friend find it, and to Jane that was more than enough.

"Did bumface confess Pet?" Marg asked.

Jane nodded. "Apparently this is the third time the house was about to be repossessed by the bank,"

"Really pet?"

"Yes, Willy Anne was tens of thousands of pounds in debt so she needed the money. She couldn't get a loan without it apparently becoming a public scandal so she stole rare books,"

Marg shook her head. "How Pet? We saw the real covers, didn't we?"

"In a way," Jane said, "We saw extremely good fakes, Willy Anne has a friend in Portsmouth that makes them. She gives the friend the original book, he makes a fake cover for her and he sells it,"

Marg nodded and shuffled down the path a little bit more. "But pet, I would know my book had been stolen?"

Jane and Marg started to walk down the path towards the beautiful dirty road and to Jane's little red car.

"But Marg, you were insured. Willy had a conscience of sorts, she knew rare book collectors never open books. You were insured so she would lose it, you would get the money and she wouldn't have to pay the friend to make a fake cover,"

Marg stopped and looked at the book in her hand. "Found it in a desk draw in another room Pet. Not sure I want it now,"

Jane pulled her friend in for a tight hug. "Yea you do. That's what your husband would have wanted, and as you said he's an evil haunter,"

Jane and Marg just laughed as they continued walking down the path, and Jane felt a massive wave of excitement wash over her as she had solved the case, put a bad woman away and most importantly protected her best friend.

She loved Marg as much as a friend could, and Jane would never ever let something bad happen to her, so as they both got into Jane's little red car and drove away. Jane knew she was going to make sure Marg got back safely, and then she was going to have a long old read.

After a great day like this, Jane needed to remember what all the fuss about books was again.

And that got her really, really excited.

MYSTERY SHORT STORY COLLECTION VOLUME 2

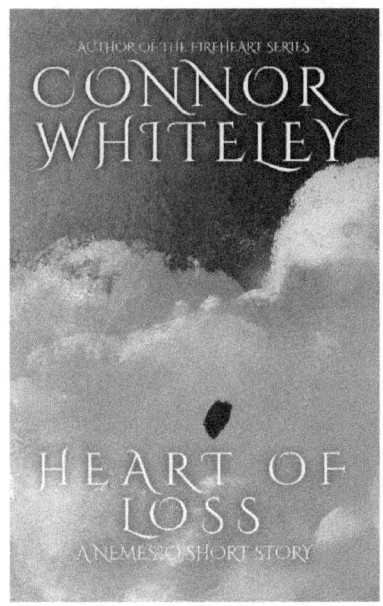

GET YOUR FREE AND EXCLUSIVE SHORT STORY NOW! LEARN ABOUT NEMESIO'S PAST!

https://www.subscribepage.com/fireheart

Keep up to date with exclusive deals on Connor Whiteley's Books, as well as the latest news about new releases and so much more!

Sign up for the Grab a Book and Chill Monthly newsletter, and you'll get one **FREE** ebook just for signing up: Agents of The Emperor Collection.

Sign Up Now!

https://dl.bookfunnel.com/f4p5xkprbk

About the author:

Connor Whiteley is the author of over 60 books in the sci-fi fantasy, nonfiction psychology and books for writer's genre and he is a Human Branding Speaker and Consultant.

He is a passionate warhammer 40,000 reader, psychology student and author.

Who narrates his own audiobooks and he hosts The Psychology World Podcast.

All whilst studying Psychology at the University of Kent, England.

Also, he was a former Explorer Scout where he gave a speech to the Maltese President in August 2018 and he attended Prince Charles' 70th Birthday Party at Buckingham Palace in May 2018.

Plus, he is a self-confessed coffee lover!

OTHER SHORT STORIES BY CONNOR WHITELEY

Blade of The Emperor
Arbiter's Truth
The Bloodied Rose
Asmodia's Wrath
Heart of A Killer
Emissary of Blood
Computation of Battle
Old One's Wrath
Puppets and Masters
Ship of Plague
Interrogation
Edge of Failure
One Way Choice
Acceptable Losses
Balance of Power
Good Idea At The Time
Escape Plan
Escape In The Hesitation
Inspiration In Need
Singing Warriors
Dragon Coins
Dragon Tea
Dragon Rider
Knowledge is Power
Killer of Polluters

MYSTERY SHORT STORY COLLECTION VOLUME 2

Climate of Death
Sacrifice of the Soul
Heart of The Flesheater
Heart of The Regent
Heart of The Standing
Feline of The Lost
Heart of The Story
The Family Mailing Affair
Defining Criminality
The Martian Affair
A Cheating Affair
The Little Café Affair
Mountain of Death
Prisoner's Fight
Claws of Death
Bitter Air
Honey Hunt
Blade On A Train
City of Fire
Awaiting Death
Poison In The Candy Cane
Christmas Innocence
You Better Watch Out
Christmas Theft
Trouble In Christmas
Smell of The Lake
Problem In A Car

Theft, Past and Team
Embezzler In The Room
A Strange Way To Go
A Horrible Way To Go
Ann Awful Way To Go
An Old Way To Go
A Fishy Way To Go
A Pointy Way To Go
A High Way To Go
A Fiery Way To Go
A Glassy Way To Go
A Chocolatey Way To Go
Kendra Detective Mystery Collection Volume 1
Kendra Detective Mystery Collection Volume 2
Stealing A Chance At Freedom
Glassblowing and Death
Theft of Independence
Cookie Thief
Marble Thief
Book Thief
Art Thief
Mated At The Morgue
The Big Five Whoopee Moments
Stealing An Election
Mystery Short Story Collection Volume 1

Mystery Short Story Collection Volume 2

Other books by Connor Whiteley:
Bettie English Private Eye Series
A Very Private Woman
The Russian Case
A Very Urgent Matter
A Case Most Personal
Trains, Scots and Private Eyes
The Federation Protects

The Fireheart Fantasy Series
Heart of Fire
Heart of Lies
Heart of Prophecy
Heart of Bones
Heart of Fate

City of Assassins (Urban Fantasy)
City of Death
City of Marytrs
City of Pleasure
City of Power

Agents of The Emperor
Return of The Ancient Ones
Vigilance
Angels of Fire
Kingmaker

The Garro Series- Fantasy/Sci-fi
GARRO: GALAXY'S END
GARRO: RISE OF THE ORDER
GARRO: END TIMES
GARRO: SHORT STORIES
GARRO: COLLECTION
GARRO: HERESY
GARRO: FAITHLESS
GARRO: DESTROYER OF WORLDS
GARRO: COLLECTIONS BOOK 4-6
GARRO: MISTRESS OF BLOOD
GARRO: BEACON OF HOPE
GARRO: END OF DAYS

Winter Series- Fantasy Trilogy Books
WINTER'S COMING
WINTER'S HUNT
WINTER'S REVENGE
WINTER'S DISSENSION

Miscellaneous:
RETURN
FREEDOM
SALVATION
Reflection of Mount Flame
The Masked One
The Great Deer

All books in 'An Introductory Series':
BIOLOGICAL PSYCHOLOGY 3RD EDITION
COGNITIVE PSYCHOLOGY THIRD EDITION
SOCIAL PSYCHOLOGY- 3RD EDITION
ABNORMAL PSYCHOLOGY 3RD EDITION
PSYCHOLOGY OF RELATIONSHIPS- 3RD EDITION
DEVELOPMENTAL PSYCHOLOGY 3RD EDITION
HEALTH PSYCHOLOGY
RESEARCH IN PSYCHOLOGY
A GUIDE TO MENTAL HEALTH AND TREATMENT AROUND THE WORLD- A GLOBAL LOOK AT DEPRESSION
FORENSIC PSYCHOLOGY
THE FORENSIC PSYCHOLOGY OF

THEFT, BURGLARY AND OTHER CRIMES AGAINST PROPERTY
CRIMINAL PROFILING: A FORENSIC PSYCHOLOGY GUIDE TO FBI PROFILING AND GEOGRAPHICAL AND STATISTICAL PROFILING.
CLINICAL PSYCHOLOGY
FORMULATION IN PSYCHOTHERAPY
PERSONALITY PSYCHOLOGY AND INDIVIDUAL DIFFERENCES
CLINICAL PSYCHOLOGY REFLECTIONS VOLUME 1
CLINICAL PSYCHOLOGY REFLECTIONS VOLUME 2
CULT PSYCHOLOGY
Police Psychology

www.ingramcontent.com/pod-product-compliance
Lightning Source LLC
LaVergne TN
LVHW011854060526
838200LV00054B/4324